Typewriter

Yevgenia Nayberg

CREATIVE EDITIONS

FRAGILE

Text and illustrations copyright © 2020 by Yevgenia Nayberg
Edited by Amy Novesky; designed by Rita Marshall, with Yevgenia Nayberg
Published in 2020 by Creative Editions P.O. Box 227, Mankato, MN 56002 USA
Creative Editions is an imprint of The Creative Company www.thecreativecompany.us
Library of Congress Cataloging-in-Publication Data
Names: Nayberg, Yevgenia, author, illustrator. Title: Typewriter / by Yevgenia Nayberg.
Summary: A neglected Russian typewriter clicks, clacks, and rings to life with a new
owner. Identifiers: LCCN 2019029591 / ISBN 978-1-56846-344-5
Subjects: CYAC: Typewriters—Fiction. / Authors—Fiction. / Immigrants—Fiction.
Classification: LCC PZ7.1.N375 Typ 2020 / DDC [E]—dc23

First edition 9 8 7 6 5 4 3 2 1

I am an old Russian typewriter.

I have keys with letters from the Russian alphabet:

 looks like a beetle.

 looks like a broom.

 looks like an apple.

I have thirty more letters to choose from!

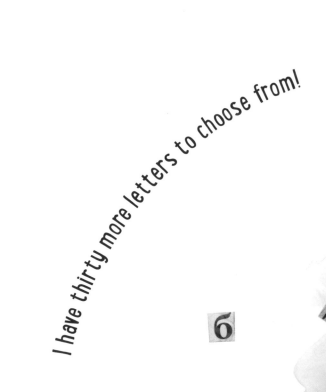

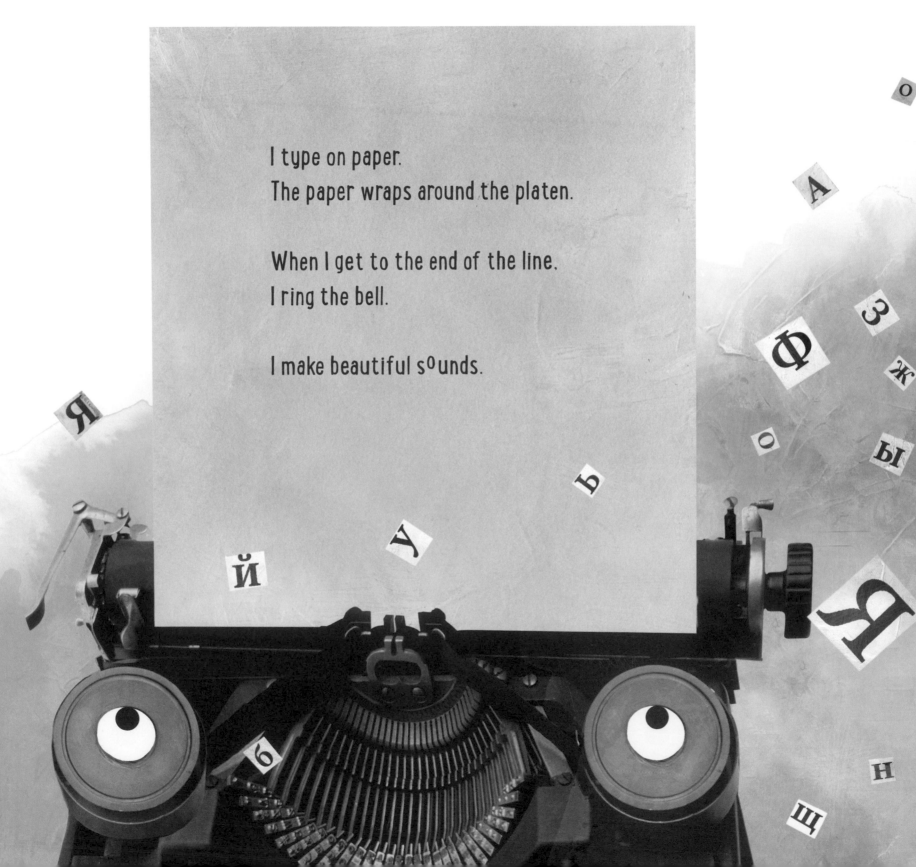

I type on paper.
The paper wraps around the platen.

When I get to the end of the line,
I ring the bell.

I make beautiful s°unds.

I once made beautiful sounds with my writer.
I met him in Russia, when I was just out of the factory, bright and shiny.

Sometimes the writer would pace back and forth around his study and talk to himself.
Other times he would stare at me and whistle quietly.
Around noon he would storm out, grab some tea, and run back in.
This is what writers do.

When the writer decided to move to America, he could only bring the most necessary things.
The writer did not want to take his pillow or blanket.
He did not even want to take his coat. He only wanted to take me!

"All I need is my Russian typewriter," the writer said.
"How else can I write in America?"

I was very heavy.
The writer huffed as he dragged me onto the plane.
I sat on his lap through the ten-hour flight
as he typed a new story.

My keys clicked and clacked. The passengers moaned and complained.

But in America, the writer did not have any time to write.

He was busy...

Scrubbing floors.

5th Street

3rd Street

Prospect Pa

CAUTION

WET
FLOO

And I collected dust.

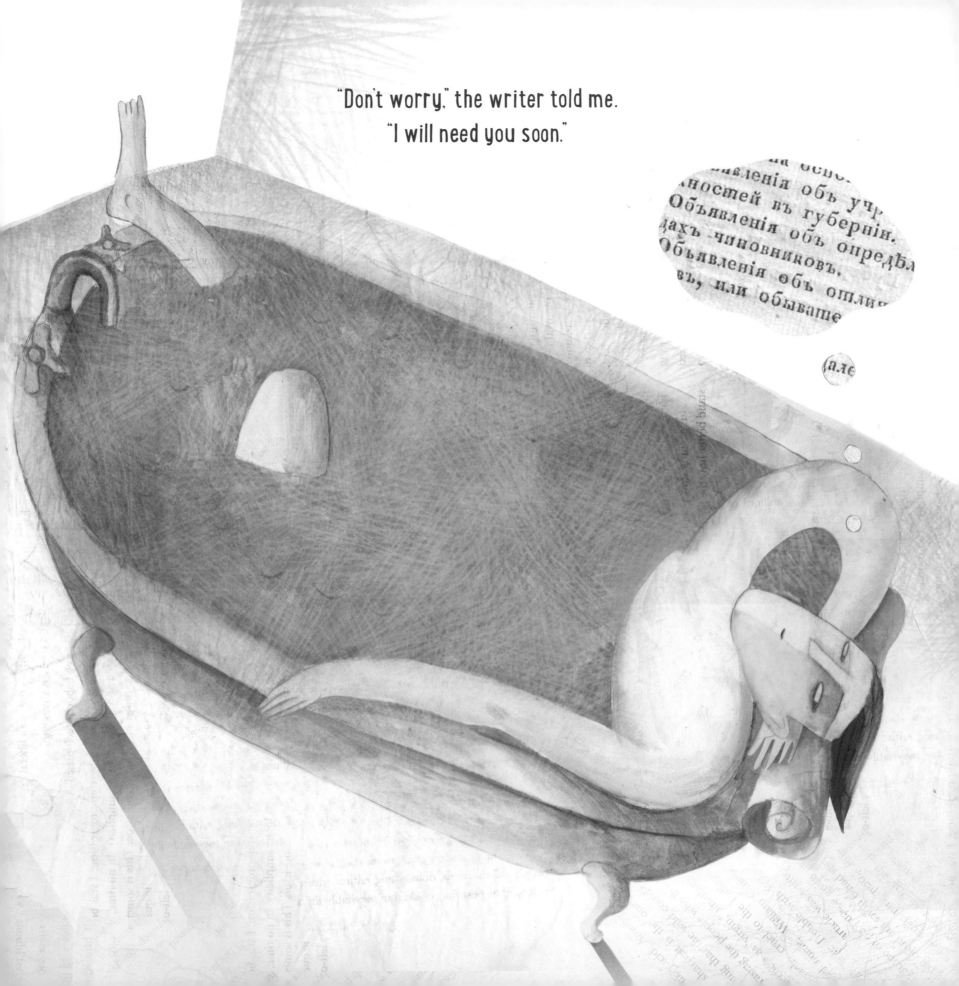

For our first American anniversary, the writer brought home something new.
It was called a laptop. The laptop had both Russian and English letters.

The laptop and I did not get along.

The writer started to write again. He took the laptop to the coffee shop.
"All American writers work on their novels at coffee shops." the writer explained.

Instead of tea, he now drank coffee.

I stayed home and collected more dust.

One day the writer walked over to my shelf.
He looked embarrassed. "I am sorry," he said.
"I must give you away. You are no longer useful."

When night came, the writer took me out to the curb.
He scribbled a note and rolled it inside my platen.

Who would want a useless typewriter?
The night was cold and silent. I felt all alone in the world.

I had read enough Russian novels to know that it would

It did.

begin to rain now.

I woke to the sound of voices.
"Dad, can we take it home?" one voice said.
A little girl and her father were standing in front of me.
"It is useless," her father said. "We don't even know Russian."
"It won't be useless to me," the girl said. "I promise!"

apartment.

to their

me upstairs

as he carried

Dad huffed

The girl pressed my shiny keys.
The platen cracked like an old tram.
The paper waved like a sail.
I typed my favorite letters for the girl.

looks like a beetle.

 looks like a broom.

 looks like an apple.

There are thirty more letters
I am going to teach her!

We will make beautiful sounds together.

рокого распро
революции. Способ
обный, портативный пат
льню. Верный попутчик р
важные речи, этот перено
овой песне, оживить вечер
и новое содержание в будни
колачивая колхозы и обобщ
взглянул на «Виктролу»
мофонную фабрику, хв
пластинок, а я..
нный мир.
пластинки
изве

Author's Note

Every immigrant family, including my own, has a story about a useful thing they brought to America, tools of the trade that doctors, artists, writers carefully packed into their suitcases after saying goodbye to their native country. My mom, an artist, brought several books on plants and birds—just in case she ever needs to look one up! I brought my grandfather's surgical scalpel to sharpen pencils.

In this story, a Russian writer brings his typewriter to America. The Russian language uses the Cyrillic alphabet, developed in the 9th century by two Greek brothers and based on the Greek alphabet. Originally, the Russian alphabet contained 43 letters! Fortunately, it has only 33 today.

If you are lucky enough to stumble upon a typewriter, make sure to press its keys. Perhaps it will make beautiful sounds for you, too!

To start typing, insert a sheet of paper into the carriage. The paper rolls around a platen. With each click of a key, the lever brings a letter stamp, called a type hammer, toward an inked ribbon. The type hammer presses the paper through the ribbon. The letter impression is left on the paper. When you release the key, the type hammer falls back into place, and the paper carriage moves one space to the left, ready for the next letter. When the end of the line is reached, the bell sounds. Now it is time to press the carriage return lever to turn the paper and start a new line.